"My American Spirit"

This publication is dedicated to my family: Valerie and Oliver (Cowboy O.)

This is the copyright page for my "My American Spirit" historical workbook.

Copyright © 2009

Cover design and book design by Neil Perry
All rights reserved.

Neil Perry
Printed in the United States of America

First Printing: March 2009

Visit website at:

www.ouramericanspirit.com

Contents

Introduction

The influences for this publication came from a few different directions. The first is when my son was born. I wanted him to have the tools in which to build his American Spirit. The beliefs that it had great meaning to know he was an American citizen. He was going to be a citizen of the greatest country this world has ever seen. Born in a land where he could dream any dream and have the greatest chance to actually make those dreams a reality. My desire is for him to be possessed by the spirit we all had on September 12, 2001. Not a spirit of fear or anger, but the spirit and belief that the American people can conquer challenges of any type. Secondly, over the last two years, we have gone through a political season that has told us and our children how bad we have it in America. I wanted to put a stop to that belief. We need to believe, as Ronald Regan and other great presidents did, that Americans can overcome anything. Just get out of our way.

Being a veteran of the US Navy, I understand the importance of remembering how we came to be, and continue to stay, a free nation. Through my meditations on the subject, I became perplexed by our country's state of mind. It seems to take a national tragedy, political season, or national holiday to bring out our American Spirit. I wondered if we had gotten back to being who we were on September 10, 2001.

During my enlistment, I was fortunate enough to have been stationed with a few Texans. I know they were Texans because they told me. As if they were getting paid to tell me. They were loud and proud. I wonder if all Americans believed in this country as much as Texans believe in Texas, would September 11th have ever happened? With this, I decided my son is not the only one that could use some help on how to be a spirited, real American.

This book is also an interactive publication. In many sections, you will provide the information. This will give you and your family the opportunity and the tools needed to take ownership of your own American Spirit.

To some, this book may seem too simple. That's the intention. I did not want this to be just another history book that no one reads. It is designed to spark more interest and provide an opportunity for you and your family to do further research together. I encourage you to use these tools to educate, to teach, and to live in "American Spirit."

The definition of "Americanism" was promulgated by the Commander-in-Chief of the Grand Army of the Republic, United Spanish War Veterans, Veterans of Foreign Wars of the United States, the National Commanders of the American Legion and the Disabled American Veterans of the World War at a conference held in Washington, in February 1927:

"Americanism is an unfailing love of country; loyalty to its institutions and ideals; eagerness to defend it against all enemies; undivided allegiance to the flag; and a desire to secure the blessings of liberty to ourselves and posterity." (Congressional Charter and By-Laws and Manual of Procedure and Ritual Veterans of Foreign Wars of the United States Podium Edition.)

Seems the worst thing for our country is to go through a presidential election campaign. It is really harmful to our nation to listen to all these candidates tell us how bad everything is for the two years it's now taking to elect a president. So, turn the television off, pick up this book and get back familiar with just how great we are. Because it is "We the People" that make this country great, not those that tell us how much we need them to make America great again. I wasn't sure we ever stopped being great. The people didn't go away, so neither has our greatness.

Also, let us not forget how big of a part God is to the greatness of America. He's not in our constitution and on our money for no reason. The founding fathers saw fit to place Him in the highest esteem as our creator:

"We hold these truths to be self-evident, that all men are created equal, that they are endowed by their Creator with certain unalienable Rights, that among these are Life, Liberty and the pursuit of Happiness."

As previously mentioned, this book is designed to be interactive. To be used as a tool to continue to build your American Spirit. You will find many tasks to research and document information. Jot down this information in the area selected. Your first task is to write down the web address from which you purchased this book.

WWW. _____

_____

Oh, thank you for purchasing this book. I hope you find this to be a good tool for you and/or your family.

Pass It On

If you, like I, feel this workbook is going to be a good tool for you and/or your family. Do you think it might be for your friends, extended family, and neighbors as well? If so, pass it on. Not your book, keep it. From here, take down the names and contact info (email address, or phone) of those with who you would like to share. Then send an email or phone message giving them the web link from which you got this book:

_____

_____

_____

_____

_____

_____

_____

_____

My American Spirit

Renew Your Mind

The renewal of your mind means not only to make a decision to see something from a different angle, but to have your second nature thinking changed as well. This happens not overnight, but daily. Below is something that we can recite, on a daily basis, to thrust us forward down the path of renewing our minds:

> "I pledge allegiance to the Flag
>
> of the United States of America
>
> and to the Republic for which it stands,
>
> one nation under God, indivisible,
>
> with liberty and justice for all."

Say you don't need a renewing? Take a few minutes to answer these questions that might be found on the United States Citizenship test. Find the answers and write them down under the questions.

United States Citizenship Test *(partial)*

1. How many houses of Congress are there? _____

2. What are they called?

   _____

   _____

3. What are the 1st 10 amendments to The Constitution called?

   _____

4. How many stars are there on the American Flag? _____

5. Who was the 1st President of the United States?

   _____

6. How long is the term of the President? _____

7. How many terms can they serve?

   _____

8. How many branches of government are there and what are they called?

_____

_____

_____

9. What is the highest court in the country?

_____

10. Who is your mayor? _____

11. How many Senators are there? _____

12. How many amendments to the Constitution are there? _____

13. When was the Declaration of Independence signed?_____

14. Who elects the President of the United States?_____

15. Who elects the Congress?_____

16. Who said, "Give me liberty or give me death."?_____

17. Who has the power to declare the war?_____

18. How many original states were there?_____

19. What are the original states names?_____

_____

_____

_____

Find a few more questions on your own:

_____

_____

_____

_____

_____

_____

_____

_____

Symbols of Freedom

The US Flag

No one knows for sure who designed the first flag. It is believed that Congressman Francis Hopkinson was most likely the designer, and few historians believe that Betsy Ross, a Philadelphia seamstress, made the first one. There are thirteen stripes, alternating red and white. Each stripe represents one of the thirteen original colonies. There are fifty stars, one for each of the United States. There are nine rows of stars. Every other row has six and five stars beginning with six stars on the top row.

Flag Etiquette

Federal law stipulates many aspects of flag etiquette. The section of law dealing with American Flag etiquette is generally referred to as the Flag Code. Some general guidelines from the Flag Code answer many of the most common questions:

- The flag should be lighted at all times, either by sunlight or by an appropriate light source.

- The flag should be flown in fair weather, unless the flag is designed for inclement weather use.

- The flag should never be dipped to any person or thing. It is flown upside down only as a distress signal.

- The flag should not be used for any decoration in general. Bunting of blue, white and red stripes is available for these purposes. The blue stripe of the bunting should be on the top.

- The flag should never be used for any advertising purpose. It should not be embroidered, printed or otherwise impressed on such articles as cushions, handkerchiefs, napkins, boxes, or anything intended to be discarded after temporary use. Advertising signs should not be attached to the staff or halyard.

- The flag should not be used as part of a costume or athletic uniform, except that a flag patch may be used on the uniform of military personnel, fireman, policeman and members of patriotic organizations.

- The flag should never have any mark, insignia, letter, word, number, figure, or drawing of any kind placed on it, or attached to it.

- The flag should never be used for receiving, holding, carrying, or delivering anything.

- When the flag is lowered, no part of it should touch the ground or any other object; it should be received by waiting hands and arms. To store the flag it should be folded neatly and ceremoniously.

- The flag should be cleaned and mended when necessary.

- When a flag is so worn it is no longer fit to serve as a symbol of our country, it should be destroyed by burning in a dignified manner.

Mount Rushmore

The four figures carved in stone on Mount Rushmore represent the first 150 years of American history. The birth of our nation was guided by the vision and courage of George Washington. Thomas Jefferson always had dreams of something bigger, first in the words of the Declaration of Independence and later in the expansion of our nation through the Louisiana Purchase. Preservation of the union was paramount to Abraham Lincoln but a nation where all men were free and equal was destined to be. At the turn of the Twentieth Century Theodore Roosevelt saw a possibility of greatness in our nation. Our nation was changing from a rural republic to a world power. The ideals of these presidents laid a foundation for our nation as solid as the rock from which their figures are carved.

Bald Eagle

The bald eagle was chosen June 20, 1782 as the emblem of the United States of America, because of its long life, great strength and majestic looks, and also because it was then believed to exist only on this continent.

The Liberty Bell

On July 8, 1776, with the Liberty Bell ringing out from the tower of Pennsylvania State House (now known as Independence Hall) summoning citizens to hear the first public reading of the Declaration of Independence by Colonel John Nixon. The bell now resides in Independence Hall in Philadelphia.

The Statue of Liberty

In 1886 the statue of "Liberty Enlightening the World" was unveiled on Bedloe's Island in the harbor of New York. The statue was the gift of the people of the republic of France to the people of the republic of the United States. The idea originated with Monsieur Bartholdi, a citizen of France, and the gift was made in recognition of the grateful love for America.

American Presidents

In this section, research to locate the names of the Vice Presidents, write their name on the blank provided.

1. George Washington, 1789-1797

    _____

2. John Adams, 1797-1801

    _____

3. Thomas Jefferson, 1801-1809

    _____

4. James Madison, 1809-1817

    _____

5. James Monroe, 1817-1825

    _____

6. John Quincy Adams, 1825-1829

    _____

7. Andrew Jackson, 1829-1837

    _____

8. Martin Van Buren, 1837-1841

    _____

9. William Henry Harrison, 1841

    _____

10.John Tyler, 1841-1845

_____

11.James Knox Polk, 1845-1849

_____

12.Zachary Taylor, 1849-1850

_____

13.Millard Fillmore, 1850-1853

_____

14.Franklin Pierce, 1853-1857

_____

15.James Buchanan, 1857-1861

_____

16.Abraham Lincoln, 1861-1865

_____

17.Andrew Johnson, 1865-1869

_____

18.Ulysses Simpson Grant, 1869-1877

_____

19.Rutherford Birchard Hayes, 1877-1881

_____

20.James Abram Garfield, 1881

_____

21. Chester Alan Arthur, 1881-1885

_____

22. Grover Cleveland, 1885-1889

_____

23. Benjamin Harrison, 1889-1893

_____

24. Grover Cleveland, 1893-1897

_____

25. William McKinley, 1897-1901

_____

26. Theodore Roosevelt, 1901-1909

_____

27. William Howard Taft, 1909-1913

_____

28. Woodrow Wilson, 1913-1921

_____

29. Warren Gamaliel Harding, 1921-1923

_____

30. Calvin Coolidge, 1923-1929

_____

31. Herbert Clark Hoover, 1929-1933

_____

32. Franklin Delano Roosevelt, 1933-1945

_____

33. Harry S. Truman, 1945-1953

_____

34. Dwight David Eisenhower 1953-1961

_____

35. John Fitzgerald Kennedy, 1961-1963

_____

36. Lyndon Baines Johnson, 1963-1969

_____

37. Richard Milhous Nixon, 1969-1974

_____

38. Gerald Rudolph Ford, 1974-1977

_____

39. James Earl Carter, Jr., 1977-1981

_____

40. Ronald Wilson Reagan, 1981-1989

_____

41. George Herbert Walker Bush, 1989-1993

_____

42. William Jefferson Clinton, 1993-2001

_____

43. George Walker Bush, 2001-2008

_____

44. Barack Hussein Obama, *2008-*

_____

List your favorite presidents:

_____

_____

_____

_____

_____

_____

_____

_____

Songs of Patriots

This should be a fun activity for you and your family. Have your children or friends or relatives children help with this one. Find the words, write them down and learn to sing them. You might bring back some old school days memories that will give you a smile.

_____

_____

_____

_____

_____

_____

_____

_____

_____

Songs of Patriots *(cont)*

_____

_____

_____

_____

_____

_____

_____

_____

_____

_____

_____

Songs of Patriots (cont)

Songs of Patriots *(cont)*

Songs of Patriots (cont)

Celebrating America

Serving this country, as a sailor in the world's finest navy, was not an easy task. However, it is considered a real blessing from God. (Can I still say that?) My eyes were opened to the beauty of our country. I got to view such things as The Grand Canyon from 30,000ft as I flew from home in Lawrenceburg, Tennessee back to San Diego, California. I experienced the homecoming celebration that San Francisco gave us via the Golden Gate and Bay Bridges' when we returned from our six month deployment to The Persian Gulf. Oh the rain in Seattle........but have you seen the Ho Rain Forest? What about MT. Rainier? Or the Cascade Mountain ranges? I could go on and on about Denver, Wyoming, Chicago, Florida, Texas, Alabama, Washington D.C., North and South Carolina,………

Our country is worth celebrating. Take the time to learn and teach why we celebrate each holiday.

Memorial Day

Memorial Day, originally called Decoration Day, is a day of remembrance for those who have died in our nation's service. There are many stories as to its actual beginnings, with over two-dozen cities and towns laying claim to being the birthplace of Memorial Day. There is also evidence that organized women's groups in the South were decorating graves before the end of the Civil War: a hymn published in 1867, "Kneel Where Our Loves are Sleeping" by Nella L. Sweet carried the dedication "To The Ladies of the South who are Decorating the Graves of the Confederate Dead" While Waterloo N.Y. was officially declared the birthplace of Memorial Day by President Lyndon Johnson in May 1966, it's difficult to prove conclusively the origins of the day. It is more likely that it had many separate beginnings; each of those towns and every planned or spontaneous gathering of people to honor the war dead in the 1860's tapped into the general human need to honor our dead, each contributed honorably to the growing movement that culminated in General Logan giving his official proclamation in 1868. It is not important who was the very first, what is important is that Memorial Day was established. Memorial Day is not about division. It is about reconciliation; it is about coming together to honor those who gave their all.

Memorial Day was officially proclaimed on May 5th 1868 by General John Logan, national commander of the Grand Army of the Republic, in his General Order No. 11, and was first observed on May 30th 1868, when flowers were placed on the graves of Union and Confederate soldiers at Arlington National Cemetery. The first state to officially recognize the holiday was New York in 1873. By 1890 it was recognized by all of the northern states. The South refused to acknowledge the day, honoring their dead on separate days until after World War I (when the holiday changed from honoring just those who died fighting in the Civil War to honoring Americans who died fighting in any war). It is now celebrated in almost every State on the last Monday in May (passed by Congress with the National Holiday Act of 1971 (P.L. 90 - 363) to ensure a three day weekend for Federal holidays), though several southern states have an additional separate day for honoring the Confederate war dead: January 19 in Texas; April 26 in Alabama, Florida, Georgia, and Mississippi; May 10 in South Carolina; and June 3 (Jefferson Davis' birthday) in Louisiana and Tennessee.

In 1915, inspired by the poem "In Flanders Fields," Moina Michael replied with her own poem:

> We cherish too, the
>
> Poppy red
>
> That grows on fields
>
> where valor led,
>
> It seems to signal to
>
> the skies
>
> That blood of heroes
>
> never dies.

She then conceived of an idea to wear red poppies on Memorial day in honor of those who died serving the nation during war. She was the first to wear one, and sold poppies to her friends and co-workers with the money going to benefit servicemen in need. Later a Madam Guerin from France was visiting the United States and learned of this new custom started by Ms.Michael and when she returned to France, made artificial red poppies to raise money for war orphaned children and widowed women. This tradition spread to other countries. In 1921, the Franco-American Children's League sold poppies nationally to benefit war orphans of France and Belgium. The League disbanded a year later and Madam Guerin approached the VFW for help. Shortly before Memorial Day in 1922 the VFW became the first veterans' organization to nationally sell poppies. Two years later their "Buddy" Poppy program was selling artificial poppies made by disabled veterans. In 1948 the US Post Office honored Ms Michael for her role in founding the National Poppy movement by issuing a red 3 cent postage stamp with her likeness on it.

"...gather around their sacred remains and garland the passionless mounds above them with choicest flowers of springtime....let us in this solemn presence renew our pledges to aid and assist those whom they have left among us as sacred charges upon the Nation's gratitude,--the soldier's and sailor's widow and orphan." --General

John Logan, General Order No. 11, 5 May 1868

- by visiting cemeteries and placing flags or flowers on the graves of our fallen heroes.

- by visiting memorials.

- by flying the U.S. Flag at half-staff until noon.

- by flying the 'POW/MIA Flag' as well (Section 1082 of the 1998 Defense Authorization Act).

- by participating in a "National Moment of Remembrance": at 3 p.m. to pause and think upon the true meaning of the day, and for Taps to be played.

- by renewing a pledge to aid the widows, widowers, and orphans of our fallen dead, and to aid the disabled veterans.

Flag Day

Inspired by decades of local and state celebrations, Flag Day - the anniversary of the Flag Resolution of 1777 - was officially *established* by the Proclamation of President Woodrow Wilson on May 30th, 1916. While Flag Day was celebrated in various communities for years after Wilson's proclamation, it was not until August 3rd, 1949, that President Truman

signed an Act of Congress designating June 14th of each year as National

Flag Day.

Veterans Day

Official recognition of the end of the first modern global conflict --
World War I - - was made in a concurrent resolution (44 Stat. 1982) enacted
by Congress on June 4, 1926, with these words:

WHEREAS the 11th of November 1918, marked the cessation of the most

destructive, sanguinary, and far reaching war in human annals and the

resumption by the people of the United States of peaceful relations with

other nations, which we hope may never again be severed, and

WHEREAS it is fitting that the recurring anniversary of this date should

be commemorated with thanksgiving and prayer and exercises designed to

perpetuate peace through good will and mutual understanding between

nations; and

WHEREAS the legislatures of twenty-seven of our States have already

declared November 11 to be a legal holiday: Therefore be it Resolved by

the Senate (the House of Representatives concurring), That the President of
the

United States is requested to issue a proclamation calling upon the officials
to

display the flag of the United States on all Government

buildings on November 11 and inviting the people of the United States to

observe the day in schools and churches, or other suitable places, with

appropriate ceremonies of friendly relations with all other peoples.

An Act (52 Stat. 351; 5 U. S. Code, Sec. 87a) approved May 13, 1938, and

the 11th of November in each year a legal holiday - - a day to be

dedicated to the cause of world peace and to be hereafter celebrated and

known as "Armistice Day. "

Armistice Day was primarily a day set aside to honor veterans of World

War I, but in 1954, after World War II had required the greatest

mobilization of soldiers, sailors, marines and airmen in the Nation's

history; after American forces had fought aggression in Korea, the 83rd

Congress, at the urging of the veterans service organizations, amended

the Act of 1938 by striking out the word "Armistice" and inserting in

lieu thereof the word "Veterans. " With the approval of this legislation

(Public Law 380) on June 1, 1954, November 11th became a day to honor

American veterans of all wars.

Later that same year, on October 8th, President Dwight D. Eisenhower

issued the first "Veterans Day Proclamation " which stated:

"In order to insure proper and widespread observance of this anniversary, all veterans, all veterans' organizations, and the entire citizenry will wish to join hands in the common purpose. Toward this end, I am designating the Administrator of Veterans' Affairs as Chairman of a Veterans Day National Committee, which shall include such other persons as the Chairman may select, and which will coordinate at the national level necessary planning for the observance. I am also requesting the heads of all departments and agencies of the Executive branch of the Government to assist the National Committee in every way possible."

July 4th

Independence Day is the national holiday of the United States of America, commemorating the signing of the Declaration of Independence by the Continental Congress on July 4, 1776, in Philadelphia, Pennsylvania.

Fireworks and July 4th

The earliest settlers brought their love of fireworks to the New World, where firings of black powder were used to celebrate holidays and impress the natives. By the time of the American Revolution, fireworks had long played a part in celebrating important events. It was natural that not only John Adams, but also many of his countrymen, should think of fireworks when Independence was declared. The very first celebration of

Independence Day was in 1777, six years before Americans knew whether the new nation would even survive the war, and fireworks were a part of the revels.

Columbus Day

The discovery of America, by Christopher Columbus, happened before dawn, on October 12, 1492, when the lookout of the "Pinta" shouted "Tierra! Tierra! This happy news came when the dauntless explorer was almost ready to give in to his men's demands that he turn back and give up the expedition. Today, Columbus Day is a holiday in the United States, and in many parts of the world including Central and South American countries. In Italy and Spain, Columbus is especially honored.

Thanksgiving

The first day of thanks in America was celebrated in Virginia at Cape Henry in 1607, but it was the Pilgrims' three-day feast celebrated in early November of 1621, which we now popularly regard as the "First Thanksgiving.

George Washington did set November 26th of 1789 Thanksgiving Day. But it was Abe Lincoln who declared the fourth Thursday of November Thanksgiving Day.

Martin Luther King Jr.

Dr. King was a perfect example of someone filled with American Spirit. We should all be a reminded to live in freedom and allow others to do the same. Martin Luther King Jr. day is celebrated on January 19th. I think it's important that all Americans understand that he was not trying to provide a path of entitlement to any one group of people but equality based upon their character not ethnicity. Take the time to find this speech. Read and meditate on the contents. Even if you've read it before, do it again. I will help you with and internal hope and belief that if you, the individual, has take care of building up personal character and that society as a whole allows for the opportunity for success, then you can do for yourself. He is some space provided so you can take down your own thoughts about the MLK's meaning.

_____

_____

_____

_____

_____

Martin Luther King Jr. (cont)

Citizenship

I believe there are three things a person can do to support this free nation: vote, military service and chose to be captured by what our freedoms really are. Free to be the hard working backbone of this nation. Free to be the job creator. Free to change your mind about religion, politics, and whom you think has the best baseball team. So, chose the American Spirit of freedom everyday.

Vote

For most of us, this is the most important patriotic activity we can do. Don't be fooled into thinking that getting registered to vote, then going to vote on the assigned local, state, and national election days is an easy process. Too many of us have become lazy when it comes to educating ourselves about the political process. The television and talk radio have provided an avenue of ignorance toward this process. Don't mistake my meaning here. I watch television and listen to talk radio. I've received good information from both. Talk radio maybe the very thing that is keeping the checks and balances going in Washington DC. Overall, these resources are businesses. They recognize that truth sells. The fact still remains that profits are the top priority. Ronald Regan said it best: "Trust but verify." Below are a few websites that offer directions to the voting records of our representatives in Washington. You will need to research to see if your local and state governments have postings of voting records.

http://www.Factcheck.org http://www.senate.gov/ http://www.senate.gov/

http://www.usa.gov/Citizen/Topics/Voting.shtml

Military Service

There can be no nation without the protection provided for by armed services. I thank God everyday that I live in the country that possesses the smartest, toughest military the world has ever seen. A mighty military and a people with a stubborn resolve for freedom, is why no other nation could ever come close to conquering The United States of America.

I served seven years in The United States Navy. I met some of the best people I had and will ever meet. It also gave me an education about America and the world. Traveling overseas taught me just how good we have it in the states. If you're young and not sure what direction you want to take in life, the military might just be the place you find those answers. I recommend seeking counsel from your local recruiter along with those around you that have served or are serving now.

Please find, write down and learn these military hymns and celebrate these dates in honor of those that are serving and served before them.

Us Navy Birthday

October 4th

US Navy Hymn

_____

_____

_____

_____

_____

_____

_____

_____

_____

US Marine Corps Birthday

November 10th

Marine Corps Hymn

US Army Birthday

June 14

Army Hymn

_____

_____

_____

_____

_____

_____

_____

_____

_____

USAF Birthday

September 18th

Air Force Hymn

_____

_____

_____

_____

_____

_____

_____

_____

_____

_____

US Coast Guard

Aug. 4, 1790

US Coast Guard Hymn

_____

_____

_____

_____

_____

_____

_____

_____

_____

_____

_____

_____

Democracy or Republic?

*"I pledge allegiance to the flag of the United States of America, and to the **Republic** for which it stands, one Nation under God, indivisible, with liberty and justice for all."*

This assignment is one of clarification. All of us have heard and most know the "pledge of allegiance" more than our favorite song. However, do we understand what it is saying? What is that word, "Republic?" What does it mean? How does it differ from a democracy? Define the two under their headings, finally, compare the differences.

Democracy:

_____

_____

_____

_____

_____

_____

_____

_____

_____

_____

_____

Republic:

_____

_____

_____

_____

_____

_____

_____

_____

_____

Difference between Democracy and Republic:

_____

_____

_____

_____

_____

_____

_____

_____

_____

_____

_____

_____

Capitalism vs. Socialism

Our country's values have been promoted through a capitalistic or free enterprise system. But what is it? What is socialism? What is the difference between the two?   Take down a few simple definitions and compare the two.

Capitalism is:

_____

_____

_____

_____

_____

_____

_____

Socialism is:

_____

_____

_____

_____

_____

_____

_____

Differences between capitalism and socialism

_____

_____

_____

_____

IN CONGRESS, JULY 4, 1776

The unanimous Declaration of the thirteen United States of America

When in the Course of human events it becomes necessary for one people to dissolve the political bands which have connected them with another and to assume among the powers of the earth, the separate and equal station to which the Laws of Nature and of Nature's God entitle them, a decent respect to the opinions of mankind requires that they should declare the causes which impel them to the separation.

We hold these truths to be self-evident, that all men are created equal, that they are endowed by their Creator with certain unalienable Rights, that among these are Life, Liberty and the pursuit of Happiness. --That to secure these rights, Governments are instituted among Men, deriving their just powers from the consent of the governed, --That whenever any Form of Government becomes destructive of these ends, it is the Right of the People to alter or to abolish it, and to institute new Government, laying its foundation on such principles and organizing its powers in such form, as to them shall seem most likely to effect their Safety and Happiness. Prudence, indeed, will dictate that Governments long established should not be changed for light and transient causes; and accordingly all experience hath shewn that mankind are more disposed to suffer, while evils are sufferable than to right themselves by abolishing the forms to which they are accustomed. But when a long train of abuses and usurpations, pursuing invariably the same Object evinces a design to reduce them under absolute Despotism, it is their right, it is their duty, to throw off such Government, and to provide new Guards for their future security. --Such has been the patient sufferance of these Colonies; and such is now the necessity which constrains them to alter their former Systems of Government. The history of the present King of Great Britain is a history of repeated injuries and usurpations, all having in direct object the establishment of an absolute Tyranny over these States. To prove this, let Facts be submitted to a candid world.

He has refuted his Assent to Laws, the most wholesome and necessary for the public good.

He has forbidden his Governors to pass Laws of immediate and pressing importance, unless suspended in their operation till his Assent should be obtained; and when so suspended, he has utterly neglected to attend to them.

He has refused to pass other Laws for the accommodation of large districts of people, unless those people would relinquish the right of Representation in the Legislature, a right inestimable to them and formidable to tyrants only.

He has called together legislative bodies at places unusual, uncomfortable, and distant from the depository of their Public Records, for the sole purpose of fatiguing them into compliance with his measures.

He has dissolved Representative Houses repeatedly, for opposing with manly firmness his invasions on the rights of the people.

He has refused for a long time, after such dissolutions, to cause others to be elected, whereby the Legislative Powers, incapable of Annihilation, have returned to the People at large for their exercise; the State remaining in the mean time exposed to all the dangers of invasion from without, and convulsions within.

He has endeavoured to prevent the population of these States; for that purpose obstructing the Laws for Naturalization of Foreigners; refusing to pass others to encourage their migrations hither, and raising the conditions of new Appropriations of Lands.

He has obstructed the Administration of Justice by refusing his Assent to Laws for establishing Judiciary Powers.

He has made Judges dependent on his Will alone for the tenure of their offices, and the amount and payment of their salaries.

He has erected a multitude of New Offices, and sent hither swarms of Officers to harass our people and eat out their substance.

He has kept among us, in times of peace, Standing Armies without the Consent of our legislatures.

He has affected to render the Military independent of and superior to the Civil Power.

He has combined with others to subject us to a jurisdiction foreign to our constitution, and unacknowledged by our laws; giving his Assent to their Acts of pretended Legislation:

For quartering large bodies of armed troops among us:

For protecting them, by a mock Trial from punishment for any Murders which they should commit on the Inhabitants of these States:

For cutting off our Trade with all parts of the world:

For imposing Taxes on us without our Consent:

For depriving us in many cases, of the benefit of Trial by Jury:

For transporting us beyond Seas to be tried for pretended offences:

For abolishing the free System of English Laws in a neighbouring Province, establishing therein an Arbitrary government, and enlarging its Boundaries so as to render it at once an example and fit instrument for introducing the same absolute rule into these Colonies

For taking away our Charters, abolishing our most valuable Laws and altering fundamentally the Forms of our Governments:

For suspending our own Legislatures, and declaring themselves invested with power to legislate for us in all cases whatsoever.

He has abdicated Government here, by declaring us out of his Protection and waging War against us.

He has plundered our seas, ravaged our Coasts burnt our towns, and destroyed the lives of our people.

He is at this time transporting large Armies of foreign Mercenaries to compleat the works of death, desolation, and tyranny, already begun with circumstances of Cruelty & Perfidy scarcely paralleled in the most barbarous ages, and totally unworthy the Head of a civilized nation.

He has constrained our fellow Citizens taken Captive on the high Seas to bear Arms against their Country, to become the executioners of their friends and Brethren, or to fall themselves by their Hands.

He has excited domestic insurrections amongst us, and has endeavoured to bring on the inhabitants of our frontiers, the merciless Indian Savages whose known rule of warfare, is an undistinguished destruction of all ages, sexes and conditions.

In every stage of these Oppressions We have Petitioned for Redress in the most humble terms: Our repeated Petitions have been answered only by repeated injury. A Prince, whose character is thus marked by every act which may define a Tyrant, is unfit to be the ruler of a free people.

Nor have We been wanting in attentions to our British brethren. We have warned them from time to time of attempts by their legislature to extend an unwarrantable jurisdiction over us. We have reminded them of the circumstances of our emigration and settlement here. We have appealed to their native justice and magnanimity, and we have conjured them by the ties of our common kindred. to disavow these usurpations, which would inevitably interrupt our connections and correspondence. They too have been deaf to the voice of justice and of consanguinity. We must, therefore, acquiesce in the necessity, which denounces our Separation, and hold them, as we hold the rest of mankind, Enemies in War, in Peace Friends.

We, therefore, the Representatives of the United States of America, in General Congress, Assembled, appealing to the Supreme Judge of the world for the rectitude of our intentions, do, in the Name, and by Authority of the good People of these Colonies, solemnly publish and declare, That these United Colonies are, and of Right ought to be Free and Independent States, that they are Absolved from all Allegiance to the British Crown, and that all political connection between them and the State of Great Britain, is and ought to be totally dissolved; and that as Free and Independent States, they have full Power to levy War, conclude Peace contract Alliances, establish Commerce, and to do all other Acts and Things which Independent States may of right do. --And for the support of this Declaration, with a firm reliance on the protection of Divine Providence, we mutually pledge to each other our Lives, our Fortunes and our sacred Honor.

--John Hancock

New Hampshire:

Josiah Bartlett, William Whipple, Matthew Thornton

Massachusetts:

John Hancock, Samuel Adams, John Adams, Robert Treat Paine, Elbridge Gerry

Rhode Island:

Stephen Hopkins, William Ellery

Connecticut:

Roger Sherman, Samuel Huntington, William Williams, Oliver Wolcott

New York:

William Floyd, Philip Livingston, Francis Lewis, Lewis Morris

New Jersey:

Richard Stockton, John Witherspoon, Francis Hopkinson, John Hart, Abraham Clark

Pennsylvania:

Robert Morris, Benjamin Rush, Benjamin Franklin, John Morton, George Clymer, James Smith, George Taylor, James Wilson, George Ross

Delaware:

Caesar Rodney, George Read, Thomas McKean

Maryland:

Samuel Chase, William Paca, Thomas Stone, Charles Carroll of Carrollton

Virginia:

George Wythe, Richard Henry Lee, Thomas Jefferson, Benjamin Harrison, Thomas Nelson, Jr., Francis Lightfoot Lee, Carter Braxton

North Carolina:

William Hooper, Joseph Hewes, John Penn

South Carolina:

Edward Rutledge, Thomas Heyward, Jr., Thomas Lynch, Jr., Arthur Middleton

Georgia:

Button Gwinnett, Lyman Hall, George Walton

THE UNITED STATES CONSTITUTION

We the People of the United States, in Order to form a more perfect Union, establish Justice, insure domestic Tranquility, provide for the common defense, promote the general Welfare, and secure the Blessings of Liberty to ourselves and our Posterity, do ordain and establish this Constitution for the United States of America.

Article. I.

Section 1.

All legislative Powers herein granted shall be vested in a Congress of the United States, which shall consist of a Senate and House of Representatives.

Section. 2.

Clause 1: The House of Representatives shall be composed of Members chosen every second Year by the People of the several States, and the Electors in each State shall have the Qualifications requisite for Electors of the most numerous Branch of the State Legislature.

Clause 2: No Person shall be a Representative who shall not have attained to the Age of twenty five Years, and been seven Years a Citizen of the United

States, and who shall not, when elected, be an Inhabitant of that State in which he shall be chosen.

Clause 3: Representatives and direct Taxes shall be apportioned among the several States which may be included within this Union, according to their respective Numbers, which shall be determined by adding to the whole Number of free Persons, including those bound to Service for a Term of Years, and excluding Indians not taxed, three fifths of all other Persons. *(See Note 2)* The actual Enumeration shall be made within three Years after the first Meeting of the Congress of the United States, and within every subsequent Term of ten Years, in such Manner as they shall by Law direct. The Number of Representatives shall not exceed one for every thirty Thousand, but each State shall have at Least one Representative; and until such enumeration shall be made, the State of New Hampshire shall be entitled to chuse three, Massachusetts eight, Rhode-Island and Providence Plantations one, Connecticut five, New-York six, New Jersey four, Pennsylvania eight, Delaware one, Maryland six, Virginia ten, North Carolina five, South Carolina five, and Georgia three.

Clause 4: When vacancies happen in the Representation from any State, the Executive Authority thereof shall issue Writs of Election to fill such Vacancies.

Clause 5: The House of Representatives shall chuse their Speaker and other Officers; and shall have the sole Power of Impeachment.

Section. 3.

Clause 1: The Senate of the United States shall be composed of two Senators from each State, chosen by the Legislature thereof, *(See Note 3)* for six Years; and each Senator shall have one Vote.

Clause 2: Immediately after they shall be assembled in Consequence of the first Election, they shall be divided as equally as may be into three Classes. The Seats of the Senators of the first Class shall be vacated at the Expiration of the second Year, of the second Class at the Expiration of the fourth Year, and of the third Class at the Expiration of the sixth Year, so that one third may be chosen every second Year; and if Vacancies happen by Resignation, or otherwise, during the Recess of the Legislature of any State, the Executive thereof may make temporary Appointments until the next Meeting of the Legislature, which shall then fill such Vacancies. *(See Note 4)*

Clause 3: No Person shall be a Senator who shall not have attained to the Age of thirty Years, and been nine Years a Citizen of the United States, and who shall not, when elected, be an Inhabitant of that State for which he shall be chosen.

Clause 4: The Vice President of the United States shall be President of the Senate, but shall have no Vote, unless they be equally divided.

Clause 5: The Senate shall chuse their other Officers, and also a President pro tempore, in the Absence of the Vice President, or when he shall exercise the Office of President of the United States.

Clause 6: The Senate shall have the sole Power to try all Impeachments. When sitting for that Purpose, they shall be on Oath or Affirmation. When the President of the United States is tried, the Chief Justice shall preside: And no Person shall be convicted without the Concurrence of two thirds of the Members present.

Clause 7: Judgment in Cases of Impeachment shall not extend further than to removal from Office, and disqualification to hold and enjoy any Office of honor, Trust or Profit under the United States: but the Party convicted shall nevertheless be liable and subject to Indictment, Trial, Judgment and Punishment, according to Law.

Section. 4.

Clause 1: The Times, Places and Manner of holding Elections for Senators and Representatives, shall be prescribed in each State by the Legislature thereof; but the Congress may at any time by Law make or alter such Regulations, except as to the Places of chusing Senators.

Clause 2: The Congress shall assemble at least once in every Year, and such Meeting shall be on the first Monday in December, *(See Note 5)* unless they shall by Law appoint a different Day.

Section. 5.

Clause 1: Each House shall be the Judge of the Elections, Returns and Qualifications of its own Members, and a Majority of each shall constitute a Quorum to do Business; but a smaller Number may adjourn from day to day, and may be authorized to compel the Attendance of absent Members, in such Manner, and under such Penalties as each House may provide.

Clause 2: Each House may determine the Rules of its Proceedings, punish its Members for disorderly Behaviour, and, with the Concurrence of two thirds, expel a Member.

Clause 3: Each House shall keep a Journal of its Proceedings, and from time to time publish the same, excepting such Parts as may in their Judgment require Secrecy; and the Yeas and Nays of the Members of either House on any question shall, at the Desire of one fifth of those Present, be entered on the Journal.

Clause 4: Neither House, during the Session of Congress, shall, without the Consent of the other, adjourn for more than three days, nor to any other Place than that in which the two Houses shall be sitting.

Section. 6.

Clause 1: The Senators and Representatives shall receive a Compensation for their Services, to be ascertained by Law, and paid out of the Treasury of the United States. *(See Note 6)* They shall in all Cases, except Treason, Felony and Breach of the Peace, beprivileged from Arrest during their Attendance at the Session of their respective Houses, and in going to and returning from the same; and for any Speech or Debate in either House, they shall not be questioned in any other Place.

Clause 2: No Senator or Representative shall, during the Time for which he was elected, be appointed to any civil Office under the Authority of the United States, which shall have been created, or the Emoluments whereof shall have been encreased during such time; and no Person holding any Office under the United States, shall be a Member of either House during his Continuance in Office.

Section. 7.

Clause 1: All Bills for raising Revenue shall originate in the House of Representatives; but the Senate may propose or concur with Amendments as on other Bills.

Clause 2: Every Bill which shall have passed the House of Representatives and the Senate, shall, before it become a Law, be presented to the President of the United States; If he approve he shall sign it, but if not he shall return it, with his Objections to that House in which it shall have originated, who shall enter the Objections at large on their Journal, and proceed to reconsider it. If after such Reconsideration two thirds of that House shall agree to pass the Bill, it shall be sent, together with the Objections, to the other House, by which it shall likewise be reconsidered, and if approved by two thirds of that House, it shall become a Law. But in all such Cases the Votes of both Houses shall be determined by yeas and Nays, and the Names of the Persons voting for and against the Bill shall be entered on the Journal of each House respectively. If any Bill shall not be returned by the President within ten Days (Sundays excepted) after it shall have been presented to him, the Same shall be a Law, in like Manner as if he had signed it, unless the Congress by their Adjournment prevent its Return, in which Case it shall not be a Law.

Clause 3: Every Order, Resolution, or Vote to which the Concurrence of the Senate and House of Representatives may be necessary (except on a question of Adjournment) shall be presented to the President of the United States; and before the Same shall take Effect, shall be approved by him, or being disapproved by him, shall be repassed by two thirds of the Senate and House of Representatives, according to the Rules and Limitations prescribed in the Case of a Bill.

Section. 8.

Clause 1: The Congress shall have Power To lay and collect Taxes, Duties, Imposts and Excises, to pay the Debts and provide for the common Defence and general Welfare of the United States; but all Duties, Imposts and Excises shall be uniform throughout the United States;

Clause 2: To borrow Money on the credit of the United States;

Clause 3: To regulate Commerce with foreign Nations, and among the several States, and with the Indian Tribes;

Clause 4: To establish an uniform Rule of Naturalization, and uniform Laws on the subject of Bankruptcies throughout the United States;

Clause 5: To coin Money, regulate the Value thereof, and of foreign Coin, and fix the Standard of Weights and Measures;

Clause 6: To provide for the Punishment of counterfeiting the Securities and current Coin of the United States;

Clause 7: To establish Post Offices and post Roads;

Clause 8: To promote the Progress of Science and useful Arts, by securing for limited Times to Authors and Inventors the exclusive Right to their respective Writings and Discoveries;

Clause 9: To constitute Tribunals inferior to the supreme Court;

Clause 10: To define and punish Piracies and Felonies committed on the high Seas, and Offences against the Law of Nations;

Clause 11: To declare War, grant Letters of Marque and Reprisal, and make Rules concerning Captures on Land and Water;

Clause 12: To raise and support Armies, but no Appropriation of Money to that Use shall be for a longer Term than two Years;

Clause 13: To provide and maintain a Navy;

Clause 14: To make Rules for the Government and Regulation of the land and naval Forces;

Clause 15: To provide for calling forth the Militia to execute the Laws of the Union, suppress Insurrections and repel Invasions;

Clause 16: To provide for organizing, arming, and disciplining, the Militia, and for governing such Part of them as may be employed in the Service of the United States, reserving to the States respectively, the Appointment of the Officers, and the Authority of training the Militia according to the discipline prescribed by Congress;

Clause 17: To exercise exclusive Legislation in all Cases whatsoever, over such District (not exceeding ten Miles square) as may, byCession of particular States, and the Acceptance of Congress, become the Seat of the Government of the United States, and to exercise like Authority over all Places purchased by the Consent of the Legislature of the State in which the Same shall be, for the Erection of Forts, Magazines, Arsenals, dock-Yards, and other needful Buildings;--And

Clause 18: To make all Laws which shall be necessary and proper for carrying into Execution the foregoing Powers, and all other Powers vested by this Constitution in the Government of the United States, or in any Department or Officer thereof.

Section. 9.

Clause 1: The Migration or Importation of such Persons as any of the States now existing shall think proper to admit, shall not be prohibited by the Congress prior to the Year one thousand eight hundred and eight, but a Tax or duty may be imposed on such Importation, not exceeding ten dollars for each Person.

Clause 2: The Privilege of the Writ of Habeas Corpus shall not be suspended, unless when in Cases of Rebellion or Invasion the public Safety may require it.

Clause 3: No Bill of Attainder or ex post facto Law shall be passed.

Clause 4: No Capitation, or other direct, Tax shall be laid, unless in Proportion to the Census or Enumeration herein before directed to be taken. *(See Note 7)*

Clause 5: No Tax or Duty shall be laid on Articles exported from any State.

Clause 6: No Preference shall be given by any Regulation of Commerce or Revenue to the Ports of one State over those of another: nor shall Vessels bound to, or from, one State, be obliged to enter, clear, or pay Duties in another.

Clause 7: No Money shall be drawn from the Treasury, but in Consequence of Appropriations made by Law; and a regular Statement and Account of the Receipts and Expenditures of all public Money shall be published from time to time.

Clause 8: No Title of Nobility shall be granted by the United States: And no Person holding any Office of Profit or Trust under them, shall, without the Consent of the Congress, accept of any present, Emolument, Office, or Title, of any kind whatever, from any King, Prince, or foreign State.

Section. 10.

Clause 1: No State shall enter into any Treaty, Alliance, or Confederation; grant Letters of Marque and Reprisal; coin Money; emit Bills of Credit; make any Thing but gold and silver Coin a Tender in Payment of Debts; pass any Bill of Attainder, ex post facto Law, or Law impairing the Obligation of Contracts, or grant any Title of Nobility.

Clause 2: No State shall, without the Consent of the Congress, lay any Imposts or Duties on Imports or Exports, except what may be absolutely necessary for executing it's inspection Laws: and the net Produce of all Duties and Imposts, laid by any State on Imports or Exports, shall be for the Use of the Treasury of the United States; and all such Laws shall be subject to the Revision and Controul of the Congress.

Clause 3: No State shall, without the Consent of Congress, lay any Duty of Tonnage, keep Troops, or Ships of War in time of Peace, enter into any Agreement or Compact with another State, or with a foreign Power, or engage in War, unless actually invaded, or in such imminent Danger as will not admit of delay.

Article. II.

Section. 1.

Clause 1: The executive Power shall be vested in a President of the United States of America. He shall hold his Office during the Term of four Years, and, together with the Vice President, chosen for the same Term, be elected, as follows

Clause 2: Each State shall appoint, in such Manner as the Legislature thereof may direct, a Number of Electors, equal to the whole Number of Senators and Representatives to which the State may be entitled in the Congress: but no Senator or Representative, or Person holding an Office of Trust or Profit under the United States, shall be appointed an Elector.

Clause 3: The Electors shall meet in their respective States, and vote by Ballot for two Persons, of whom one at least shall not be an Inhabitant of the same State with themselves. And they shall make a List of all the

Persons voted for, and of the Number of Votes for each; which List they shall sign and certify, and transmit sealed to the Seat of the Government of the United States, directed to the President of the Senate. The President of the Senate shall, in the Presence of the Senate and House of Representatives, open all the Certificates, and the Votes shall then be counted. The Person having the greatest Number of Votes shall be the President, if such Number be a Majority of the whole Number of Electors appointed; and if there be more than one who have such Majority, and have an equal Number of Votes, then the House of Representatives shall immediately chuse by Ballot one of them for President; and if no Person have a Majority, then from the five highest on the List the said House shall in like Manner chuse the President. But in chusing the President, the Votes shall be taken by States, the Representation from each State having one Vote; A quorum for this Purpose shall consist of a Member or Members from two thirds of the States, and a Majority of all the States shall be necessary to a Choice. In every Case, after the Choice of the President, the Person having the greatest Number of Votes of the Electors shall be the Vice President. But if there should remain two or more who have equal Votes, the Senate shall chuse from them by Ballot the Vice President. *(See Note 8)*

Clause 4: The Congress may determine the Time of chusing the Electors, and the Day on which they shall give their Votes; which Day shall be the same throughout the United States.

Clause 5: No Person except a natural born Citizen, or a Citizen of the United States, at the time of the Adoption of this Constitution, shall be eligible to the Office of President; neither shall any Person be eligible to that Office who shall not have attained to the Age of thirty five Years, and been fourteen Years a Resident within the United States.

Clause 6: In Case of the Removal of the President from Office, or of his Death, Resignation, or Inability to discharge the Powers and Duties of the said Office, *(See Note 9)* the Same shall devolve on the VicePresident, and the Congress may by Law provide for the Case of Removal, Death, Resignation or Inability, both of the President and Vice President, declaring what Officer shall then act as President, and such Officer shall act accordingly, until the Disability be removed, or a President shall be elected.

Clause 7: The President shall, at stated Times, receive for his Services, a Compensation, which shall neither be encreased nor diminished during the Period for which he shall have been elected, and he shall not receive within that Period any other Emolument from the United States, or any of them.

Clause 8: Before he enter on the Execution of his Office, he shall take the following Oath or Affirmation:--"I do solemnly swear (or affirm) that I will faithfully execute the Office of President of the United States, and will to the best of my Ability, preserve, protect and defend the Constitution of the United States."

Section. 2.

Clause 1: The President shall be Commander in Chief of the Army and Navy of the United States, and of the Militia of the several States, when called into the actual Service of the United States; he may require the Opinion, in writing, of the principal Officer in each of the executive Departments, upon any Subject relating to the Duties of their respective Offices, and he shall have Power to grant Reprieves and Pardons for Offences against the United States, except in Cases of Impeachment.

Clause 2: He shall have Power, by and with the Advice and Consent of the Senate, to make Treaties, provided two thirds of the Senators present concur; and he shall nominate, and by and with the Advice and Consent of the Senate, shall appoint Ambassadors, other public Ministers and Consuls, Judges of the supreme Court, and all other Officers of the United States, whose Appointments are not herein otherwise provided for, and which shall be established by Law: but the Congress may by Law vest the Appointment of such inferior Officers, as they think proper, in the President alone, in the Courts of Law, or in the Heads of Departments.

Clause 3: The President shall have Power to fill up all Vacancies that may happen during the Recess of the Senate, by granting Commissions which shall expire at the End of their next Session.

Section. 3.

He shall from time to time give to the Congress Information of the State of the Union, and recommend to their Consideration such Measures as he shall judge necessary and expedient; he may, on extraordinary Occasions, convene both Houses, or either of them, and in Case of Disagreement between them, with Respect to the Time of Adjournment, he may adjourn them to such Time as he shall think proper; he shall receive Ambassadors and other public Ministers; he shall take Care that the Laws be faithfully executed, and shall Commission all the Officers of the United States.

Section. 4.

The President, Vice President and all civil Officers of the United States, shall be removed from Office on Impeachment for, and Conviction of, Treason, Bribery, or other high Crimes and Misdemeanors.

Article. III.

Section. 1.

The judicial Power of the United States, shall be vested in one supreme Court, and in such inferior Courts as the Congress may from time to time ordain and establish. The Judges, both of the supreme and inferior Courts, shall hold their Offices during good Behaviour, and shall, at stated Times, receive for their Services, a Compensation, which shall not be diminished during their Continuance in Office.

Section. 2.

Clause 1: The judicial Power shall extend to all Cases, in Law and Equity, arising under this Constitution, the Laws of the United States, and Treaties made, or which shall be made, under their Authority;--to all Cases affecting Ambassadors, other public Ministers and Consuls;--to all Cases of admiralty and maritime Jurisdiction;--to Controversies to which the United States shall be a Party;--to Controversies between two or more States;--between a State and Citizens of another State; *(See Note 10)*--between Citizens of different States, --between Citizens of the same State claiming Lands under Grants of different States, and between a State, or the Citizens thereof, and foreign States, Citizens or Subjects.

Clause 2: In all Cases affecting Ambassadors, other public Ministers and Consuls, and those in which a State shall be Party, the supreme Court shall have original Jurisdiction. In all the other Cases before mentioned, the supreme Court shall have appellate Jurisdiction, both as to Law and Fact, with such Exceptions, and under such Regulations as the Congress shall make.

Clause 3: The Trial of all Crimes, except in Cases of Impeachment, shall be by Jury; and such Trial shall be held in the State where the said Crimes shall have been committed; but when not committed within any State, the Trial shall be at such Place or Places as the Congress may by Law have directed.

Section. 3.

Clause 1: Treason against the United States, shall consist only in levying War against them, or in adhering to their Enemies, giving them Aid and Comfort. No Person shall be convicted of Treason unless on the Testimony of two Witnesses to the same overt Act, or on Confession in open Court.

Clause 2: The Congress shall have Power to declare the Punishment of Treason, but no Attainder of Treason shall work Corruption of Blood, or Forfeiture except during the Life of the Person attainted.

Article. IV.

Section. 1.

Full Faith and Credit shall be given in each State to the public Acts, Records, and judicial Proceedings of every other State. And the Congress may by general Laws prescribe the Manner in which such Acts, Records and Proceedings shall be proved, and the Effect thereof.

Section. 2.

Clause 1: The Citizens of each State shall be entitled to all Privileges and Immunities of Citizens in the several States.

Clause 2: A Person charged in any State with Treason, Felony, or other Crime, who shall flee from Justice, and be found in another State, shall on Demand of the executive Authority of the State from which he fled, be delivered up, to be removed to the State having Jurisdiction of the Crime.

Clause 3: No Person held to Service or Labour in one State, under the Laws thereof, escaping into another, shall, in Consequence of any Law or Regulation therein, be discharged from such Service or Labour, but shall be delivered up on Claim of the Party to whom such Service or Labour may be due. *(See Note 11)*

Section. 3.

Clause 1: New States may be admitted by the Congress into this Union; but no new State shall be formed or erected within the Jurisdiction of any other State; nor any State be formed by the Junction of two or more States, or Parts of States, without the Consent of the Legislatures of the States concerned as well as of the Congress.

Clause 2: The Congress shall have Power to dispose of and make all needful Rules and Regulations respecting the Territory or other Property belonging to the United States; and nothing in this Constitution shall be so construed as to Prejudice any Claims of the United States, or of any particular State.

Section. 4.

The United States shall guarantee to every State in this Union a Republican Form of Government, and shall protect each of them against Invasion; and on Application of the Legislature, or of the Executive (when the Legislature cannot be convened) against domestic Violence.

Article. V.

The Congress, whenever two thirds of both Houses shall deem it necessary, shall propose Amendments to this Constitution, or, on the Application of the Legislatures of two thirds of the several States, shall call a Convention for proposing Amendments, which, in either Case, shall be valid to all Intents and Purposes, as Part of this Constitution, when ratified by the Legislatures of three fourths of the several States, or by Conventions in three fourths thereof, as the one or the other Mode of Ratification may be proposed by the Congress; Provided that no Amendment which may be made prior to the Year One thousand eight hundred and eight shall in any Manner affect the first and fourth Clauses in the Ninth Section of the first Article; and that no State, without its Consent, shall be deprived of its equal Suffrage in the Senate.

Article. VI.

Clause 1: All Debts contracted and Engagements entered into, before the Adoption of this Constitution, shall be as valid against the United States under this Constitution, as under the Confederation.

Clause 2: This Constitution, and the Laws of the United States which shall be made in Pursuance thereof; and all Treaties made, or which shall be made, under the Authority of the United States, shall be the supreme Law of the Land; and the Judges in every State shall be bound thereby, any Thing in the Constitution or Laws of any State to the Contrary notwithstanding.

Clause 3: The Senators and Representatives before mentioned, and the Members of the several State Legislatures, and all executive and judicial

Officers, both of the United States and of the several States, shall be bound by Oath or Affirmation, to support this Constitution; but no religious Test shall ever be required as a Qualification to any Office or public Trust under the United States.

Article. VII.

The Ratification of the Conventions of nine States, shall be sufficient for the Establishment of this Constitution between the States so ratifying the Same.

done in Convention by the Unanimous Consent of the States present the Seventeenth Day of September in the Year of our Lord one thousand seven hundred and Eighty seven and of the Independence of the United States of America the Twelfth In witness whereof We have hereunto subscribed our Names,

GO WASHINGTON--President and deputy from Virginia [Signed also by the deputies of twelve States.]

Delaware

Geo: Read

Gunning Bedford

jun

John Dickinson

Richard Bassett

Jaco: Broom

Maryland

James MCHenry

Dan of ST ThoS.

Jenifer

DanL Carroll.

Virginia

John Blair--

James Madison Jr.

North Carolina

WM Blount

RichD. Dobbs

Spaight.

Hu Williamson

South Carolina

J. Rutledge

Charles

1ACotesworth

Pinckney

Charles Pinckney

Pierce Butler.

Georgia

William Few

Abr Baldwin

New Hampshire

John Langdon

Nicholas Gilman

Massachusetts

Nathaniel Gorham

Rufus King

Connecticut	Pennsylvania
WM. SamL. Johnson	B Franklin
Roger Sherman	Thomas Mifflin
	RobT Morris
New York	Geo. Clymer
	ThoS. FitzSimons
Alexander Hamilton	Jared Ingersoll
	James Wilson.
New Jersey	Gouv Morris
Wil: Livingston	**Attest William**
David Brearley.	**Jackson**
WM. Paterson.	**Secretary**
Jona: Dayton	

Bill of Rights in the United States of America

Articles in addition to, and amendment of, The Constitution of the United States of America, proposed by Congress, and ratified by the legislatures of the several states pursuant to the fifth article of the original Constitution.

The first 10 amendments to the Constitution were proposed by the Congress on Sept. 25, 1789. They were ratified by the following states, and the notifications of the ratification by the governors thereof were successively communicated by the President to the Congress: New Jersey, Nov. 20, 1789; Maryland, Dec. 19, 1789; North Carolina, Dec. 22, 1789; South Carolina, Jan. 19, 1790; New Hampshire, Jan. 25, 1790; Delaware, Jan. 28, 1790; New York, Feb. 4, 1790; Pennsylvania, March 10, 1790; Rhode Island, June 7, 1790; Vermont, Nov. 3, 1791; and Virginia, Dec. 15, 1791. Ratification was completed on Dec. 15, 1791.

The amendments were subsequently ratified by Massachusetts, March 2, 1939; Georgia, March 18, 1939; and Connecticut, April 19, 1939.

Two other amendments were concurrently proposed in 1789. One failed of ratification. The other (Amendment XXVII) was not ratified until May 7, 1992, when the Michigan legislature gave it the required number of state approvals.

Amendment [I]

Congress shall make no law respecting an establishment of religion, or prohibiting the free exercise thereof; or abridging the freedom of speech, or of the press; or the right of the people peaceably to assemble, and to petition the Government for a redress of grievances.

Amendment [II]

A well regulated Militia, being necessary to the security of a free State, the right of the people to keep and bear Arms, shall not be infringed.

Amendment [III]

No Soldier shall, in time of peace be quartered in any house, without the consent of the Owner, nor in time of war, but in a manner to be prescribed by law.

Amendment [IV]

The right of the people to be secure in their persons, houses, papers, and effects, against unreasonable searches and seizures, shall not be violated, and no Warrants shall issue, but upon probable cause, supported by Oath or affirmation, and particularly describing the place to be searched, and the persons or things to be seized.

Amendment [V]

No person shall be held to answer for a capital, or otherwise infamous crime, unless on a presentment or indictment of a Grand Jury, except in cases arising in the land or naval forces, or in the Militia, when in actual service in time of War or public danger; nor shall any person be subject for the same offence to be twice put in jeopardy of life or limb; nor shall be compelled in any criminal case to be a witness against himself, nor be deprived of life, liberty, or property, without due process of law; nor shall private property be taken for public use without just compensation.

Amendment [VI]

In all criminal prosecutions, the accused shall enjoy the right to a speedy and public trial, by an impartial jury of the State and district wherein the crime shall have been committed, which district shall have been previously ascertained by law, and to be informed of the nature and cause of the accusation; to be confronted with the witnesses against him; to have compulsory process for obtaining Witnesses in his favor, and to have the assistance of counsel for his defense.

Amendment [VII]

In Suits at common law, where the value in controversy shall exceed twenty dollars, the right of trial by jury shall be preserved, and no fact tried by a jury, shall be otherwise reexamined in any Court of the United States, than according to the rules of the common law.

Amendment [VIII]

Excessive bail shall not be required, nor excessive fines imposed, nor cruel and unusual punishments inflicted.

Amendment [IX]

The enumeration in the Constitution, of certain rights, shall not be construed to deny or disparage others retained by the people.

Amendment [X]

The powers not delegated to the United States by the Constitution, nor prohibited by it to the States, are reserved to the States respectively, or to the people.

Amendment [XI] [1795]

The Judicial power of the United States shall not be construed to extend to any suit in law or equity, commenced or prosecuted against one of the United States by Citizens of another State, or by Citizens or Subjects of any Foreign State.

Amendment [XII] [1804]

The electors shall meet in their respective states and vote by ballot for President and Vice President, one of whom, at least, shall not be an inhabitant of the same state with themselves; they shall name in their ballots the person voted for as President, and in distinct ballots the person voted for as Vice President, and they shall make distinct lists of all persons voted for as President, and of all persons voted for as Vice President, and of the number of votes for each, which lists they shall sign and certify, and transmit sealed to the seat of the government of the United States, directed to the President of the Senate;

—The President of the Senate shall, in the presence of the Senate and House of Representatives, open all the certificates and the votes shall then be counted;

— The person having the greatest number of votes for President, shall be the President, if such number be a majority of the whole number of Electors appointed;

and if no person have such majority, then from the persons having the highest numbers not exceeding three on the list of those voted for as President, the House of Representatives shall choose immediately, by ballot, the President. But in choosing the President, the votes shall be taken by states, the representation from each state having one vote; a quorum for this purpose shall consist of a member or members from two-thirds of the states, and a majority of all the states shall be necessary to a choice.

[And if the House of Representatives shall not choose a President whenever the right of choice shall devolve upon them, before the fourth day of March next following, then the Vice President shall act as President, as in the case of the death or other constitutional disability of the President.]

The person having the greatest number of votes as Vice President, shall be the Vice President, if such number be a majority of the whole number of Electors appointed, and if no person have a majority, then from the two highest numbers on the list, the Senate shall choose the Vice President; a quorum for the purpose shall consist of two-thirds of the whole number of Senators, and a majority of the whole number shall be necessary to a choice. But no person constitutionally ineligible to the office of President shall be eligible to that of Vice President of the United States.

Amendment XIII [1865]

Section 1

Neither slavery nor involuntary servitude, except as punishment for crime whereof the party shall have been duly convicted, shall exist within the United States, or any place subject to their jurisdiction.

Section 2

Congress shall have power to enforce this article by appropriate legislation.

Amendment XIV [1868]

Section 1

All persons born or naturalized in the United States, and subject to the jurisdiction thereof, are citizens of the United States and of the State wherein they reside. No State shall make or enforce any law which shall abridge the privileges or immunities of citizens of the United States; nor shall any State deprive any person of life, liberty, or property, without due process of law; nor deny to any person within its jurisdiction the equal protection of the laws.

Section 2

Representatives shall be apportioned among the several States according to their respective numbers, counting the whole number of persons in each State, excluding Indians not taxed. But when the right to vote at any election for the choice of electors for President and Vice President of the United States, Representatives in Congress, the Executive and Judicial officers of a State, or the members of the Legislature thereof, is denied to any of the male inhabitants of such State, being twenty-one years of age, and citizens of the United States, or in any way abridged, except for participation in rebellion, or other crime, the basis of representation therein shall be reduced in the proportion which the number of such male citizens shall bear to the whole number of male citizens twenty-one years of age in such State.

Section 3

No person shall be a Senator or Representative in Congress, or elector of President and Vice President, or hold any office, civil or military, under the United States, or under any State, who, having previously taken an oath, as a member of Congress, or as an officer of the United States, or as a member of any State legislature, or as an executive or judicial officer of any State, to support the Constitution of the United States, shall have engaged in insurrection or rebellion against the same, or given aid or comfort to the enemies thereof. But Congress may by a vote of two-thirds of each House, remove such disability.

Section 4

The validity of the public debt of the United States, authorized by law, including debts incurred for payment of pensions and bounties for services in suppressing insurrection or rebellion, shall not be questioned. But neither the United States nor any State shall assume or pay any debt or obligation incurred in aid of insurrection or rebellion against the United States, or any claim for the loss or emancipation of any slave; but all such debts, obligations and claims shall be held illegal and void.

Section 5

The Congress shall have power to enforce, by appropriate legislation, the provisions of this article.

Amendment XV [1870]

Section 1

The right of citizens of the United States to vote shall not be denied or abridged by the United States or by any State on account of race, color, or previous condition of servitude.

Section 2

The Congress shall have power to enforce this article by appropriate legislation.

Amendment XVI [1913]

The Congress shall have power to lay and collect taxes on incomes, from whatever source derived, without apportionment among the several States, and without regard to any census or enumeration.

Amendment [XVII] [1913]

The Senate of the United States shall be composed of two Senators from each State, elected by the people thereof, for six years; and each Senator shall have one vote. The electors in each State shall have the qualifications requisite for electors of the most numerous branch of the State legislatures.

When vacancies happen in the representation of any State in the Senate, the executive authority of such State shall issue writs of election to fill such vacancies: Provided, that the legislature of any State may empower the executive thereof to make temporary appointments until the people fill the vacancies by election as the legislature may direct.

This amendment shall not be so construed as to affect the election or term of any Senator chosen before it becomes valid as part of the Constitution.

Amendment [XVIII] [1919]
Section 1

After one year from the ratification of this article the manufacture, sale, or transportation of intoxicating liquors within, the importation thereof into, or the exportation thereof from the United States and all territory subject to the jurisdiction thereof for beverage purposes is hereby prohibited.

Section 2

The Congress and the several States shall have concurrent power to enforce this article by appropriate legislation.

Section 3

This article shall be inoperative unless it shall have been ratified as an amendment to the Constitution by the legislatures of the several States, as provided in the Constitution, within seven years from the date of the submission hereof to the States by the Congress.

Amendment [XIX] [1920]

The right of citizens of the United States to vote shall not be denied or abridged by the United States or by any State on account of sex.

Congress shall have power to enforce this article by appropriate legislation.

Amendment [XX] [1933]

Section 1

The terms of the President and Vice President shall end at noon on the 20th day of January, and the terms of Senators and Representatives at noon on the 3d day of January, of the years in which such terms would have ended if this article had not been ratified; and the terms of their successors shall then begin.

Section 2

The Congress shall assemble at least once in every year, and such meeting shall begin at noon on the 3d day of January, unless they shall by law appoint a different day.

Section 3

If, at the time fixed for the beginning of the term of the President, the President elect shall have died, the Vice President elect shall become President. If a President shall not have been chosen before the time fixed for the beginning of his term, or if the President elect shall have failed to qualify, then the Vice President elect shall act as President until a President shall have qualified; and the Congress may by law provide for the case wherein neither a President elect nor a Vice President elect shall have qualified, declaring who shall then act as President, or the manner in which one who is to act shall be selected, and such person shall act accordingly until a President or Vice President shall have qualified.

Section 4

The Congress may by law provide for the case of the death of any of the persons from whom the House of Representatives may choose a President whenever the right of choice shall have devolved upon them, and for the case of the death of any of the persons from whom the Senate may choose a Vice President whenever the right of choice shall have devolved upon them.

Section 5

Sections 1 and 2 shall take effect on the 15th day of October following the ratification of this article.

Section 6

This article shall be inoperative unless it shall have been ratified as an amendment to the Constitution by the legislatures of three-fourths of the several States within seven years from the date of its submission.

Amendment [XXI] [1933]

Section 1

The eighteenth article of amendment to the Constitution of the United States is hereby repealed.

Section 2

The transportation or importation into any State, Territory, or possession of the United States for delivery or use therein of intoxicating liquors, in violation of the laws thereof, is hereby prohibited.

Section 3

This article shall be inoperative unless it shall have been ratified as an amendment to the Constitution by conventions in the several States, as provided in the Constitution, within seven years from the date of the submission hereof to the States by the Congress.

Amendment [XXII] [1951]

Section 1

No person shall be elected to the office of the President more than twice, and no person who has held the office of President, or acted as President, for more than two years of a term to which some other person was elected President shall be elected to the office of the President more than once. But this Article shall not apply to any person holding the office of President when this Article was proposed by the Congress, and shall not prevent any person who may be holding the office of President, or acting as President, during the term within which this Article becomes operative from holding the office of President or acting as President during the remainder of such term.

Section 2

This article shall be inoperative unless it shall have been ratified as an amendment to the Constitution by the legislatures of three-fourths of the several States within seven years from the date of its submission to the States by the Congress.

Amendment [XXIII] [1961]

Section 1

The District constituting the seat of Government of the United States shall appoint in such manner as the Congress may direct:

A number of electors of President and Vice President equal to the whole number of Senators and Representatives in Congress to which the District would be entitled if it were a State, but in no event more than the least populous State; they shall be in addition to those appointed by the States, but they shall be considered, for the purposes of the election of President and Vice President, to be electors appointed by a State; and they shall meet in the District and perform such duties as provided by the twelfth article of amendment.

Section 2

The Congress shall have power to enforce this article by appropriate legislation.

Amendment [XXIV] [1964]

Section 1

The right of citizens of the United States to vote in any primary or other election for President or Vice President, for electors for President or Vice President, or for Senator or Representative in Congress, shall not be denied or abridged by the United States or any State by reason of failure to pay any poll tax or other tax.

Section 2

The Congress shall have power to enforce this article by appropriate legislation.

Amendment [XXV] [1967]

Section 1

In case of the removal of the President from office or of his death or resignation, the Vice President shall become President.

Section 2

Whenever there is a vacancy in the office of the Vice President, the President shall nominate a Vice President who shall take office upon confirmation by a majority vote of both Houses of Congress.

Section 3

Whenever the President transmits to the President pro tempore of the Senate and the Speaker of the House of Representatives his written declaration that he is unable to discharge the powers and duties of his office, and until he transmits to them a written declaration to the contrary, such powers and duties shall be discharged by the Vice President as Acting President.

Section 4

Whenever the Vice President and a majority of either the principal officers of the executive departments or of such other body as Congress may by law provide, transmit to the President pro tempore of the Senate and the Speaker of the House of Representatives their written declaration that the President is unable to discharge the powers and duties of his office, the Vice President shall immediately assume the powers and duties of the office as Acting President.

Thereafter, when the President transmits to the President pro tempore of the Senate and the Speaker of the House of Representatives his written declaration that no inability exists, he shall resume the powers and duties of his office unless the Vice President and a majority of either the principal officers of the executive department or of such other body as Congress may by law provide, transmit within four days to the President pro tempore of the Senate and the Speaker of the House of Representatives their written declaration that the President is unable to discharge the powers and duties of his office.

Thereupon Congress shall decide the issue, assembling within forty-eight hours for that purpose if not in session. If the Congress, within twenty-one days after receipt of the latter written declaration, or, if Congress is not in session, within twenty-one days after Congress is required to assemble, determines by two-thirds vote of both Houses that the President is unable to discharge the powers and duties of his office, the Vice President shall continue to discharge the same as Acting President; otherwise, the President shall resume the powers and duties of his office.

Amendment [XXVI] [1971]

Section 1

The right of citizens of the United States, who are eighteen years of age or older, to vote shall not be denied or abridged by the United States or by any State on account of age.

Section 2

The Congress shall have power to enforce this article by appropriate legislation.

Amendment [XXVII] [1992]

No law, varying the compensation for the services of the Senators and Representatives, shall take effect, until an election of Representatives shall have intervened.

Presidential Quotes and Speeches

Below are a few quotes from past presidents. There is also some space provided to find and write down your favorite quotes.

1. "America is too great for small dreams." *Ronald Regan*

2. "He who permits himself to tell a lie once, finds it much easier to do it a second and third time, till at length it becomes habitual; he tells lies without attending to it, and truths without the world's believing him. This falsehood of the tongue leads to that of the heart, and in time depraves all its good dispositions." *Thomas Jefferson*

3. "Above all, tell the truth." *Grover Cleveland*

4. "Character is the only secure foundation of the state." Calvin Coolidge.

5. _____

6. _____

7. _____

8. _____

9. _____

10. _____

11. _____

12. _____

13. _____

14. _____

15. _____

16. _____

George Washington

First Inaugural Address (April 30, 1789) (partial)

I dwell on this prospect with every satisfaction which an ardent love for my Country can inspire: since there is no truth more thoroughly established, than that there exists in the oeconomy and course of nature, an indissoluble union between virtue and happiness, between duty and advantage, between the genuine maxims of an honest and magnanimous policy, and the solid rewards of public prosperity and felicity: Since we ought to be no less persuaded that the propitious smiles of Heaven, can never be expected on a nation that disregards the eternal rules of order and right, which Heaven itself has ordained: And since the preservation of the sacred fire of liberty, and the destiny of the Republican model of Government, are justly considered as deeply, perhaps as finally staked, on the experiment entrusted to the hands of the American people.

Gettysburg Address:

"Fourscore and seven years ago our fathers brought forth on this continent, a new nation, conceived in liberty, and dedicated to the proposition that all men are created equal. Now we are engaged in a great civil war, testing whether that nation or any nation so conceived and so dedicated can long endure. We are met on a great battlefield of that war. We have come to dedicate a portion of that field, as a final resting place for those who here gave their lives that that nation might live. It is altogether fitting and proper that we should do this. But, in a larger sense, we cannot dedicate - we cannot consecrate - we cannot hallow - this ground. The brave men, living and dead, who struggled here, have consecrated it far above our poor power to add or detract. The world will little note nor long remember what we say here, but it can never forget what they did here. It is for us, the living, rather to be dedicated here to the unfinished work which they who fought here have thus far so nobly advanced. It is rather for us to be here dedicated to the great task before us - that from these honored dead we take increased devotion to that cause for which they gave the last full measure of devotion;

that we here highly resolve that these dead shall not have died in vain; that this nation, under God, shall have a new birth of freedom; and that government of the people, by the people, for the people, shall not perish from the earth." (November 19, 1863)

Franklin D. Roosevelt - Declaration of War to Japan - December 8th 1941

Yesterday, December 7, 1941 - a date which will live in infamy - the United States of America was suddenly and deliberately attacked by naval and air forces of the Empire of Japan.

The United States was at peace with that nation, and, at the solicitation of Japan, was still in conversation with its government and its Emperor looking toward the maintenance of peace in the Pacific.

Indeed, one hour after Japanese air squadrons had commenced bombing in the American island of Oahu, the Japanese Ambassador to the United States and his colleague delivered to our Secretary of State a formal reply to a recent American message. And, while this reply stated that it seemed useless to continue the existing diplomatic negotiations, it contained no threat or hint of war or of armed attack.

It will be recorded that the distance of Hawaii from Japan makes it obvious that the attack was deliberately planned many days or even weeks ago. During the intervening time the Japanese Government has deliberately sought to deceive the United States by false statements and expressions of hope for continued peace.

The attack yesterday on the Hawaiian Islands has caused severe damage to American naval and military forces. I regret to tell you that very many American lives have been lost. In addition, American ships have been reported torpedoed on the high seas between San Francisco and Honolulu.

Yesterday the Japanese Government also launched an attack against Malaya.

Last night Japanese forces attacked Hong Kong.

Last night Japanese forces attacked Guam.

Last night Japanese forces attacked the Philippine Islands.

Last night the Japanese attacked Wake Island.

And this morning the Japanese attacked Midway Island.

Japan has therefore undertaken a surprise offensive extending throughout the Pacific area. The facts of yesterday and today speak for themselves. The people of the United States have already formed their opinions and well understand the implications to the very life and safety of our nation.

As Commander-in-Chief of the Army and Navy I have directed that all measures be taken for our defense, that always will our whole nation remember the character of the onslaught against us.

No matter how long it may take us to overcome this premeditated invasion, the American people, in their righteous might, will win through to absolute victory.

I believe that I interpret the will of the Congress and of the people when I assert that we will not only defend ourselves to the uttermost but will make it very certain that this form of treachery shall never again endanger us.

Hostilities exist. There is no blinking at the fact that our people, our territory and our interests are in grave danger.

With confidence in our armed forces, with the unbounding determination of our people, we will gain the inevitable triumph. So help us God.

I ask that the Congress declare that since the unprovoked and dastardly attack by Japan on Sunday, December 7, 1941, a state of war has existed between the United States and the Japanese Empire.

President George W Bush - 9/11 - Address to the Nation September 11th 2001

Good evening. Today, our fellow citizens, our way of life, our very freedom came under attack in a series of deliberate and deadly terrorist acts. The victims were in airplanes, or in their offices; secretaries, businessmen and women, military and federal workers; moms and dads, friends and neighbors. Thousands of lives were suddenly ended by evil, despicable acts of terror.

The pictures of airplanes flying into buildings, fires burning, huge structures collapsing, have filled us with disbelief, terrible sadness, and a quiet, unyielding anger. These acts of mass murder were intended to frighten our nation into chaos and retreat. But they have failed; our country is strong.

A great people has been moved to defend a great nation. Terrorist attacks can shake the foundations of our biggest buildings, but they cannot touch the foundation of America. These acts shattered steel, but they cannot dent the steel of American resolve.

America was targeted for attack because we're the brightest beacon for freedom and opportunity in the world. And no one will keep that light from shining.

Today, our nation saw evil, the very worst of human nature. And we responded with the best of America -- with the daring of our rescue workers, with the caring for strangers and neighbors who came to give blood and help in any way they could.

Immediately following the first attack, I implemented our government's emergency response plans. Our military is powerful, and it's prepared. Our emergency teams are working in New York City and Washington, D.C. to help with local rescue efforts.

Our first priority is to get help to those who have been injured, and to take every precaution to protect our citizens at home and around the world from further attacks.

The functions of our government continue without interruption. Federal agencies in Washington which had to be evacuated today are reopening for essential personnel tonight, and will be open for business tomorrow. Our financial institutions remain strong, and the American economy will be open for business, as well.

The search is underway for those who are behind these evil acts. I've directed the full resources of our intelligence and law enforcement communities to find those responsible and to bring them to justice. We will make no distinction between the terrorists who committed these acts and those who harbor them.

I appreciate so very much the members of Congress who have joined me in strongly condemning these attacks. And on behalf of the American people, I thank the many world leaders who have called to offer their condolences and assistance.

America and our friends and allies join with all those who want peace and security in the world, and we stand together to win the war against terrorism. Tonight, I ask for your prayers for all those who grieve, for the children whose worlds have been shattered, for all whose sense of safety and security has been threatened. And I pray they will be comforted by a power greater than any of us, spoken through the ages in Psalm 23: "Even though I walk through the valley of the shadow of death, I fear no evil, for You are with me."

This is a day when all Americans from every walk of life unite in our resolve for justice and peace. America has stood down enemies before, and we will do so this time. None of us will ever forget this day. Yet, we go forward to defend freedom and all that is good and just in our world.

Inaugural (Excerpts): JFK

Let the word go forth from this time and place, to friend and foe alike, that the torch has been passed to a new generation of Americans, born in this century, tempered by war, disciplined by a hard and bitter peace, proud of our ancient heritage, and unwilling to witness or permit the slow undoing of those human rights to which this nation has always been committed, and to which we are committed today at home and around the world. Let every nation know, whether it wishes us well or ill, that **we shall pay any price, bear any burden, meet any hardship, support any friend, oppose any foe to assure the survival and the success of liberty.** . . . Let us never negotiate out of fear, but let us never fear to negotiate. . . . **And so my fellow Americans, ask not what your country can do for you; ask what you can do for your country.**"

Presidential Oath

"I do solemnly swear (or affirm) that I will faithfully execute the office of President of the United States, and will to the best of my ability, preserve, protect and defend the Constitution of the United States."

Andrew Jackson

Bank Veto (July 10, 1832)(*partial*)

The bill "to modify and continue" the act entitled "An act to incorporate the subscribers to the Bank of the United States" was presented to me on the 4th July instant. Having considered it with that solemn regard to the principles of the Constitution which the day was calculated to inspire, and come to the conclusion that it ought not to become a law, I herewith return it to the Senate, in which it originated, with my objections.

A bank of the United States is in many respects convenient for the Government and useful to the people. Entertaining this opinion, and deeply impressed with the belief that some of the powers and privileges possessed by the existing bank are unauthorized by the Constitution, subversive of the rights of the States, and dangerous to the liberties of the people, I felt it my duty at an early period of my Administration to call the attention of Congress to the practicability of organizing an institution combining all its advantages and obviating these objections. I sincerely regret that in the act before me I can perceive none of those modifications of the bank charter which are necessary, in my opinion, to make it compatible with justice, with sound policy, or with the Constitution of our country.

References

Congressional Charter and By-Laws and Manual of Procedure and Ritual Veterans of Foreign Wars of the United States Podium Edition.

A history of the United States, Thompson, 1920

http://www.usflag.org/flag.day.html

http://www.baldeagleinfo.com/eagle/eagle9.html

www.twilightbridge.com

http://www.earthcam.com/features/july4th/2002/history.html

http://uscis.gov/graphics/exec/natz/natztest.asp

Nation of Nations. Davidson, Gienapp, Heyrman, Lytle, and Stoff. Mcgraw-Hill. 2002

http://www.nps.gov/moru/

http://www.patriotism.org/columbus_day/

Black's Law Dictionary, Fifth Edition.

CPSIA information can be obtained at www.ICGtesting.com
Printed in the USA
LVOW091259011212

309648LV00001B/2/P